Sight-Singing Manual

ALLEN IRVINE McHOSE

and

RUTH NORTHUP TIBBS

Eastman School of Music Series

THIRD EDITION

Prentice-Hall, Inc., Englewood Cliffs, New Jersey

Printed in the United States of America

ISBN: 0-13-809707-0

Library of Congress Catalog Card Number: M57-1003

10 9 8 7 6 5 4 3

ACKNOWLEDGMENTS

The authors wish to express their deepest appreciation to the following publishers for the use of melodies found in their publications. The numbers below refer to the selections by section in this volume.

Ascherberg, Hopwood & Crew Ltd., London, for 2-11 and 2-25 from *English Peasant Songs* by Frank Kidson.

Associated Music Publishers, Inc., New York, for 1-75, 1-27, 1-77, 1-84, 1-91, 1-147, 1-148, 11-2, 12-1, 12-6, 12-8, and 12-9 from *Das Lied der Völker* by Heinrich Moeller. Published by B. Schott's Söhne. For 2-20 from *Norges Melodies*, Vol. I of the Wilhelm Hansen Edition. For 1-149 from *Danmarks Melodibog*, Book I and Book III of the Wilhelm Hansen Edition.

Augener Ltd., London, for 11-33 from *The Minstrelsy of Ireland* by Alfred Moffat. For 1-36, 3-2, 11-30, 11-37, and 11-41 from *The Minstrelsy of Scotland* by Alfred Moffat.

Bayley & Ferguson, London, for 1-54, 1-56, 1-141, 1-146, and 1-158 from *The Minstrelsy of England* by Alfred Moffat.

C. C. Birchard and Company, Boston, for 6-7 and 12-37 from *Pan and the Priest* by Howard Hanson.

Chappell & Co. Ltd., London, for 2-10 and 3-24 from *Old English Ditties*, Vol. I by William Chappell.

J & W. Chester Ltd., London, for 12-4 from *Fourteen Russian Folk Songs* by Rosa Newmarch, For 12-41 from *Histoire du Soldat* by Igor Stravinsky.

J. M. Dent & Sons (Canada) Limited, Toronto, for 5-13 from *Songs and Ballads of Nova Scotia* by Helen Creighton.

The H. W. Gray Company, New York, for 11-18 from *Medieval Modes* by A. Madely Richardson.

Harcourt, Brace and Company, Inc., New York, for 3-11, 3-12, 3-10, and 5-10 from *The American Songbag* compiled by Carl Sandburg.

Harvard University Press, Cambridge, for 1-47, 5-14, 11-12, and 11-31 from *Ballads and Sea Songs of Newfoundland* by Greenleaf-Mansfield.

Howell, Soskin, Publishers, Inc., New York, for 1-21, 1-71, 1-90, 1-33, 1-143, 1-156, 2-22, 3-16, 5-2, 7-17, and 7-26 from *A Treasury of the World's Finest Folk Songs* by Leonhard Deutsch.

Alfred A. Knopf, Inc., New York, for 4-18 from *Singing Cowboy* by Margaret Larkin.

Novello & Co., Limited, London, for 6-8 from *Beyond These Voices Is Peace* by C. H. H. Parry.

Theodore Presser Co., Philadelphia, for 7-4 from *Songs from the North* by Valborg Stub. For 3-32, from *One Hundred Songs of England* edited by Granville Bantock. For 1-132, 11-14, and 11-38 from *One Hundred Folksongs of all Nations* edited by Granville Bantock. For 12-21, 12-34, and 12-36 from *Sixty Folksongs of France* by Julien Tiersot.

Charles Scribner's Sons, New York, for 7-2 and 11-13 from *English County Songs* by Lucy E. Broadwood.

The Viking Press, Inc., New York, for 5-17, 5-18, 5-20, 5-21, 5-22, 5-23, 5-25, 5-26, and 11-16 from *The Books of American Negro Spirituals* by James Weldon Johnson.

Grateful acknowledgment is made to Melvin LeMon for use of 11-20 and 12-17 from his Pennsylvania anthracite miner's folk songs, part of the dissertation requirement for the degree Doctor of Philosophy, Eastman School of Music, University of Rochester, July 1941.

PRENTICE-HALL INTERNATIONAL, INC., *London*
PRENTICE-HALL OF AUSTRALIA, PTY. LTD., *Sydney*
PRENTICE-HALL OF CANADA, LTD., *Toronto*
PRENTICE-HALL OF INDIA PRIVATE LIMITED, *New Delhi*
PRENTICE-HALL OF JAPAN, INC., *Tokyo*

Preface

This manual is a complete revision of the former *Sight-Singing Manual*. The material is organized to correlate more closely with *Basic Principles of the Technique of 18th and 19th Century Composition,* as well as with more recent textbooks concerned with the development of musicianship. In addition, this manual contains music that can be used in courses beyond the freshman year. Many of the two- and three-voice compositions could serve as examples for analysis in counterpoint courses. The fugue subjects would be extremely useful in the study of inventions and fugues.

The melodies and two- and three-voice compositions are taken from music literature of the 16th, 17th, 18th, 19th, and 20th centuries. Tempo indications, phrasing, and dynamics have been carefully applied so that the student of sight-singing may develop, from the outset, a complete understanding of the music. The form of each composition should be carefully examined.

Two new sections have been added to provide a more complete and broad experience in sight-singing. A section dealing with chromaticism contains music using altered tones within a given key or altered tones to create chromatic modulation. The other section contains music of the 16th and 17th centuries. The music selected is of two kinds: that which is purely in the 16th century style and that which serves as a bridge between 16th century music and that of the 18th and 19th centuries.

In some sections of the manual one will find short melodies under the heading of "Quickies." These melodies are either fugue subjects or thematic phrases from instrumental or vocal music. These "Quickies" will provide an excellent means for determining just how well the class has grasped the material in each section. Two- and three-voice sight-singing drills are found in most sections. Training in part-singing is developed through imitation, rather than note against note. This procedure provides greater melodic independence for each voice. For this reason, canons, fugal expositions, and other contrapuntal forms are included in the two- and three-voice music.

For further sight-singing material the authors recommend that the departments of theory equip themselves with a sufficient number of copies of the following for class participation:

The A Cappella Chorus Series—Max T. Krone and Griffith Jones
    Vol. I, II, III, IV, V, and VI
    M. Witmark and Sons, New York

The Concord Anthem Books—Archibald Davison
    Book I and Book II
    E. C. Schirmer, Boston, Mass.

The Concord Song Book for Women's Voices—Davison and Surette
    E. C. Schirmer, Boston, Mass.

The Clarendon Song Books—Whittaker
    Books 1, 2, 3, 4, 5, and 6
    Oxford Press, London
    (For each book one may obtain a piano edition)

The Folk Song Sight Singing Series
    Books I through VII
    Oxford Press, London

Experience in sight-singing recitatives and arias, as well as in part-singing, may be obtained in 18th and 19th century cantatas and oratorios.

A. I. McH.
R.N.T.

Contents

Introduction

The basic organization of the material in this manual is controlled by two factors—*rhythm* and *pitch*. The sections of this manual relating to meter are correlated with Chapters 1 through 12 of *The Basic Principles of the Technique of 18th and 19th Century Composition* by Allen McHose.

SIGHT-SINGING MANUAL		BASIC PRINCIPLES
Section I	The Beat, Meter, and Elementary Time Durations in Simple Time	Chapters 1, 2, and 3
Section II	Durations within the Compound Beat	Chapter 4
Section III	Subdivision of the Simple Beat into Four Divisions	Chapter 5
Section IV	Further Study of the Tie	Chapter 6
Section V	Syncopation	Chapter 7
Section VI	Superimposed Backgrounds and Superimposed Meters	Chapter 8
Section VII	Further Study of the Subdivision of the Background	Chapter 9
Section IX	The Divided Beat	Chapter 10
Section XII	Further Study of Meter, Mixed Meter, Polymeter, Unusual Meter	Chapters 11 and 12

This type of organization makes it possible for the instructor to emphasize rhythm in his teaching, independent of problems in pitch. It is always wise to keep rhythmic problems slightly ahead of the complexities of pitch relations in the teaching of sight-singing.

PITCH

It will be observed that Sections I, II, and III are sub-divided into small sections stressing fundamental pitch relationships. The reason for this organization is to give the student drill in certain pitch relationships but at the same time to increase gradually the difficulty of rhythmic organization. See for example, the following, which all have the same harmonic background:

> The melodies of Section I   1—42
>
> The melodies of Section II   1—9
>
> The melodies of Section III   1—10

One will find that each pitch relationship presented in *The Basic Principles of the Technique of 18th and 19th Century Composition* can be located in the early sections of the *Sight-Singing Manual,* based upon the idea of drills progressing from easy to more difficult rhythm.*

The authors urge the use of the letter names of the notes, the student thinking the accidental when it appears. This is, in reality, an adaptation of the French "Fixed Doh" system.

The authors also urge, as an absolute necessity for thorough training, the use of all four of the commonly used clefs. To begin training in the alto and tenor clefs, the instructor should have the students recite the names of the notes, using the simple exercises in Section I. For example, change a treble or bass clef to an alto clef. As soon as the student can read the lines and spaces of the alto, continue the same training, using the tenor clef.

The clef-reciting drills just described should be introduced before actual sight-singing is introduced. One will observe that both the alto and tenor clefs are introduced in the opening sections of the *Sight-Singing Manual.*

The Seven Clefs

The *staff* used today was established during the latter part of the 17th century. It is composed of five parallel lines with the four intervening spaces.† When a *clef sign* is placed on one of the five lines, each line represents a definite fixed *pitch.*

At present only three clef signs are used, those for G, C, and F:

     = g′   called *g-one*

     = c′   called *c-one*

     = f   called *small f*

The *treble clef* is represented by the *G-clef sign* on the second line of the staff. The names of the lines and spaces are:

---

* In future printings of *Basic Principles of the Technique of 18th and 19th Century Composition,* references will be made directly to the *Sight-Singing Manual.*

† A staff of four lines, dating from an earlier period, is still used for plain song notation.

The *C-clef sign* may be placed on any line except the fifth, as follows:

SOPRANO CLEF

MEZZO-SOPRANO CLEF

ALTO CLEF

TENOR CLEF

The *F-clef* sign may be placed on the third or fourth line, as follows:

BARITONE CLEF

BASS CLEF

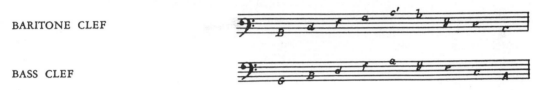

Of these seven clefs, only four are used at present: *treble, alto, tenor,* and *bass.* For this reason the melodies in this manual use only these four clefs. The student will have to read in the seven clefs, however, in connection with transposition by clefs.

Rules for Transposing by Clef

RULE I. How to select the proper clef: Locate the position of the *key-tone* (*tonic of the key,* or *final of the mode*) of the melody on the staff. Change its name to the tonic or final to which the melody will be transposed. Select the clef, and use the correct *key or modal signature* for the new *transposition center.*

ILLUSTRATION: The following last phrase of a melody in the *key of G Major* is to be transposed to the *key of E Major:*

Locate the tonic of G Major, call it E, and select the proper clef and key signature, as follows:

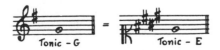

If the original melody contains *accidentals*, the student must apply the following rules in order to locate the new pitches accurately. The student must think in the new key after the new clef and signature have been adopted.

RULE IIa. If the new key has *more sharps* or *fewer flats*, find the *difference in accidentals*, take that number in the *order of the sharps* (f, c, g, d, a, e, b), and *raise one-half step* any accidental appearing before these notes as the melody is sung in the new key.

RULE IIb. If the new key has *more flats* or *fewer sharps*, find the *difference in accidentals*, take that number in the *order of the flats* (b, e, a, d, g, c, f), and *lower one-half step* any accidental appearing before these notes as the melody is sung in the new key.

ILLUSTRATION: The following example, from Pergolesi's Stabat Mater, originally in the *key of G Minor*, is to be transposed to the *key of A Minor*. The *alto clef* names the new *tonic* on the second line. The *difference in accidentals* is *two sharps*, because *fewer flats* means *raising accidentals;* consequently, any accidental appearing in the new key before f and c must be *raised one-half step*.

When transposition takes place *from flat keys to sharp keys* or *from sharp keys to flat keys,* the difference in accidentals becomes the *sum of the accidentals.*

ILLUSTRATION: The following example, from a sonata by Frederick the Great, originally in the *key of B♮ Major*, is to be transposed to the *key of E Major*. The *mezzo-soprano clef* names the new *tonic* on the third line. The *difference in accidentals* is six, and any accidental appearing in the new key before f, c, g, d, a, and e must be *raised one-half step*.

One of the accepted methods of transposition uses the seven clefs. If an instructor wishes to use this method, the student will have to learn to read in three other clefs: soprano, mezzo-soprano, and baritone. When the student is able to read in all seven clefs, then he can transpose, using the transposition Rules I, IIa, and IIb.

The Notated Appoggiatura

The appoggiatura, or leaning note, which is frequently encountered in music of the late 17th, the 18th, and the early 19th century, is as important melodically as the note to which it is attached. There are two fundamental rules for the performance of the appoggiatura:

RULE I. If the appoggiatura leans on a simple note, it absorbs half of the time value of the simple note.

RULE II. If the appoggiatura leans on a dotted note, it absorbs two-thirds of the time value of the dotted note.

Elementary Problems in Rhythm, Melodies in Major and Minor Keys with Modulations to Closely Related Keys

RHYTHMIC READING

Rhythmic reading is a special drill to give the student practice in co-ordinating the *conductor's beat* with the *time values* represented by the *notes*. The drill involves the reciting of syllables; those used in this Section are as follows:

The *beat* is assigned an Arabic numeral (1, 2, 3, etc.) depending upon the *position of the beat* in the *measure*. Example:

When *beats* are *tied*, the reciting syllable takes the name of the *beat* which originates the *tie*, and the student sounds this syllable until the *time value* has been consummated. Example:

When the *beat* is divided into *two equal time durations,** the reciting syllables are "**one-te**," "**two-te**," etc. Example:

When the *beat* is *tied* into the *equal division of the beat*, the student holds the originating syllable until its *time value* has been consummated and then recites "te."

---

* The *beat* divided into *two equal time durations* is called a *simple beat*. Meters using a *simple beat* create *simple time. Meter signatures* indicate the *number of beats* in the *measure*, and the *kind of beat*. 2/4 *meter* is called *simple duple.*

Example:

Recite: Four one ___ te three four-te one two three four   one-te two three ___ te   one

The rhythmic reading procedure is as follows:

A. Make the *conductor's beat* with the right hand.
B. Tap the *background of the beat* with the left hand, *two equal time values* for a *simple beat*.
C. Recite the *time values of the notes*, using the rhythmic syllables.

The *time values* used in this Section are as follows:

1. Symbols indicating the duration of the *beat*.
2. Symbols indicating the duration of *two or more beats*.
3. Symbols indicating the duration of *one-half the value of the beat*.
4. Symbols indicating the duration of *one or more beats tied* into the first of *two equal divisions of the beat*.

HARMONIC BACKGROUND

TONIC AND DOMINANT

Major Key

1. KONG DIDERIKS KAEMPERS FAERD I BIRTINGS LAND

Denmark

2. GESTRENGES REGIMENT

German

3. BERMER RISE OG ORM UNGERSVEND

Denmark

4. STARÝ A MLADÁ

Bohemia

5. DUKTE MANO SIMONÉNE

Lithuania

6. MIALA BABA TRZY CERY

Poland

7. SESTRA TRAVIČKA

Bohemia

8. LILLE JON

Denmark

9. SCHWABISCHES VOLKSLIED

Germany

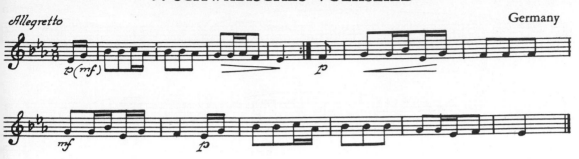

10. DIE EULE UND DER ADLER

Germany

11. A LA MODE DE FRANCE

Great Britain

12. DER BAUM IM ODENWALD

Germany

*Melodies Which Imply the V and V⁷**

13. DIE GEFANGENEN REITER

Germany

*See *Basic Principles of the Technique of 18th and 19th Century Composition,* melodic major scale, page 118.

14. ZABRAL SIE NA WOJNE

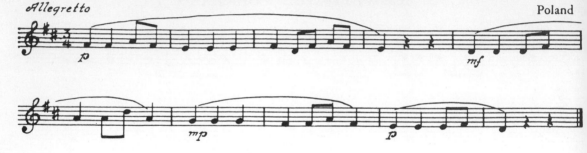

15. A LOVELY LASS TO A FRIAR CAME

16. GOLD VÖGELEIN GIEBT BESCHEID

17. DIE ARME SEELE

18. DIE STIEFMUTTER

19. PAUSE

Schubert

20. EXCERPT FROM OP. 36, NO. 1

Clementi

21. AT THE CHERRY TREE

Finland

22. MALÉ A DOSPĚLÉ DĚVČE

Bohemia

23. DO KOŚCIOLA DZWONILI

Poland

24. JA UBOGA DZIEWCZYNA

Poland

Minor Key

25. MY GOOD NEIGHBOR

Hungary

26. RADA NENÁSLEDOVANÁ

Bohemia

27. SEI NICHT BÖSE, MEIN LIEB' VÄTERLEIN!

Bohemia

28. DAR

Bohemia

29. LES OBJETS PERDUS

Piccini

30. DE MINNEBODE

France

31. VAGGVISA

Sweden

32. U MÉJ MATKI RODZONÉJ

Poland

33. HOW SHOULD I YOUR TRUE LOVE KNOW?

England

34. STOLT INGERLILLIES DØD

Denmark

35. THE SHEPHERD'S DAUGHTER

England

36. MERELLÄ SYNTYNYT

37. IT WAS A' FOR OUR RIGHTFU' KING

38. WEZMĘ JA 'ZUPAN

39. THE SHEPHERD'S DAUGHTER

40. LES GOUTS REUNIS

41. SVEND FELDINGS KAMP MED RISEN

42. ALDRAHÖGST UPPA HIMLENS FÄSTE

SUBDOMINANT AND SUPERTONIC

Major Key

43. YKSINÄINEN

44. LA ENRAMADA

45. URBANOVA NAPOJNICA

46. ISTA PJESMA

47. YOUNG BARBOUR

Newfoundland

48. KJER JE MARIJA HODILA

Slovakia

49. ROBIN HOOD AND THE BISHOP OF HEREFORD

England

50. NEDBALÝ

Bohemia

51. DER NACHTBESUCH

German

52. DER DESERTEUR

German

Sight-Singing Manual

53. HET STANDBEELD VAN

Netherlands

54. QUEEN ELEANOR'S CONFESSION

England

55. KTÓŻ TAM POD MOJÉM OKIENECZKIEM PUKA

Poland

56. ROBIN HOOD AND THE BISHOP OF HEREFORD

England

57. SKROMNA ŻADOST

58. BALLADA

59. ISTA PJESMA

60. THE LASS OF PATIE'S MILL

61. THE LITTLE DUSTMAN

SIGHT-SINGING MANUAL

62. LOVE WILL FIND OUT THE WAY

England

63. THEME FROM OP. 36, NO. 5

Clementi

64. JYDSK VISE

Norway

65. SCHEIDEN

Germany

66. DER TREUE KNABE

Germany

67. HAMBURGER MÄDCHEN

Germany

68. DROHUNG

Germany

69. CHEVY CHACE

England

70. UPRCHLÁ PASTEVNICE

Bohemia

71. IN MY YARD VIOLETS

Hungary

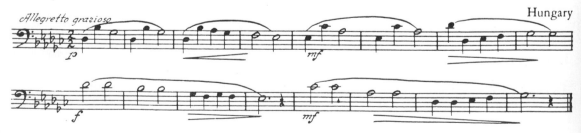

72. WHEN MY WIFE IS LAID IN GROUND

Great Britain

73. SO MACHEN SIE'S

Germany

74. DER UNERBITTLICHE HAUPTMANN

Germany

Minor Key

75. SANKT MARTIN (LEGENDE)

Denmark

76. RIBOLD OG GULDBORG

77. HANS DIE ROSSE TRÄNKTE

78. KVINDELIST

79. ITKUANI EN MÄ PITÄÄ VOI

80. DIOUGAN GWENC'HLAN

France

81. SCHLÄCHTERS TÖCHTERLEIN

Germany

82. JA JADE DO WOJNY

Poland

83. VENÄLÄISEN RAKKAUS

Finland

84. FÜLL DIE TÄLER AUS

Poland

85. THE FAIREST NYMPH

England

86. DRONNING DAGMARS DØD

Denmark

87. LASTANSA MUREHTIA AITI

Finland

88. GRIM KING OF THE GHOSTS

England

89. GO FROM MY WINDOW

England

90. ELDER BLOOMING

Russia

91. ALLERSEELEN

Poland

DOMINANT SEVENTH

Major and Minor Keys

92. DER JÄGER UND DIE SCHÄFERIN

Germany

93. GOOD-MORROW, GOSSIP JOAN

England

94. CHANSON GASCONNE

France

95. MATKA A SYNÁČEK

Bohemia

96. DEN UNGE HERR PEDERSSØN

Denmark

97. COME ROUSE, BROTHER SPORTSMEN

Great Britain

98. ZWEI KÖNIGSKINDER

Germany

99. WENN ICH EIN KLEIN'S WALDVÖGLEIN WÄR'

Germany

100. EN GANG I BREDD MED MIG

QUICKIES

Fugue Subjects

101.

Mendelssohn

102.

Fenaroli

103.

Spohr

104.

Gounod

105.

Ouseley

SECTION I

27

106.

Sala

107.

Telemann

108.

Muffat

109.

Porpora

110.

Sala

111.

Beethoven

112.

Beethoven

Themes

113.

J. S. Bach

114.

Franck

115.

Mozart

116.

Gluck

117.

Schubert

118.

Mozart

119.

Schubert

120.

Schumann

Allegro

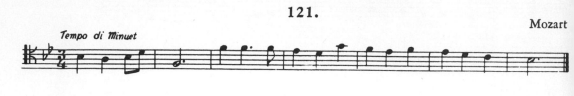

121.

Mozart

Tempo di Minuet

122.

Mozart

With spirit

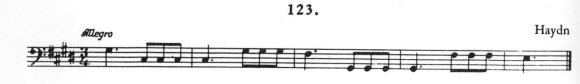

123.

Haydn

Allegro

124.

Haydn

Adagio

125.

Brahms

Allegro

126.

Berlioz

Allegretto

SIGHT-SINGING MANUAL

127.

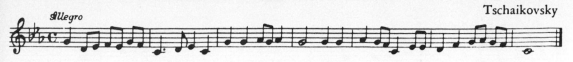

128.

Mendelssohn

129.

Rameau

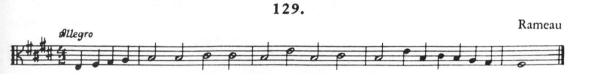

130. EXCERPT FROM OP. 18

Brahms

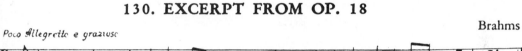

MODULATION TO CLOSELY RELATED KEYS

131. THE VICAR OF BRAY

England

132. THE TREASURE

Bohemia

133. WHERE THE GRASS IS GROWING

Moravia

134. THE OXFORDSHIRE TRAGEDY

England

135. DER ABENDSTERN

Schumann

136. FLOW GENTLY, SWEET AFTON

Scotland

137. THE JOLLY WATERMAN

England

138. GAY BACCHUS

Great Britain

139. DET HAVER SAA NYLIGEN REGNET

Denmark

140. ON THE OCEAN

Franz

* See Section VI for Rhythmic Syllables

141. WOMAN, LOVE AND WINE

England

142. NEUJAHRSLIED

143. A DEW FROM HEAVEN

144. RIPE IS THE CORN

145. GO NO MORE A RUSHING

146. TALK NOT SO MUCH TO ME OF LOVE

Webber

147. DER JÜNGLING ZOG AUS IN DEN KRIEG

Lithuania

148. MARSCHALL STIGS TÖCHTER

Denmark

149. HAR HAAND DU LAGT PAA HEERENS PLOV

A. Winding

150. AVSKJE MAE HÖVRINGEN

Norway

151. LIEBES MÄDCHEN, HÖR MIR ZU

Haydn

152. LOVE ME LITTLE, LOVE ME LONG

England

153. DREIKÖNIGSLIED

Alsace

154. SINCE THERE'S SO SMALL DIFFERENCE

Great Britain

Chorus

155. IS THERE ANY LEATHER LEFT?

Con Modo   Hungary

156. ROSE GARDEN

Germany

Allegretto grazioso

157. O THAT I HAD NEVER MARRIED

England

Plaintively, but not very slow

158. THE COUNTRY PARSON

England

Moderato

159. THE THREE RAVENS

England

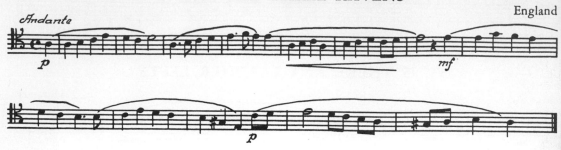

QUICKIES

Fugue Subjects

160.

Handel

161.

Rubenstein

162.

J. S. Bach

163.

Kirnberger

164.

Frescobaldi

Moderato

165.

Klengel

Andantino

166.

Handel

Moderato

167.

Handel

Maestoso

168.

Albrechtsberger

Lento

169.

Haydn

Maestoso

170.

J. S. Bach

Andante

171.

Hummel

Allegro

172.

173.

Mozart

174.

Prout

175.

Weber

176. PASSACAGLIA (THEME)

Rheinberger

TWO-VOICE COMPOSITIONS

Bass Counterpoint

177. WENN WIR IN HÖCHSTEN NÖTEN SEIN

J. S. Bach

178. AN WASSERFLÜSSEN BABYLON

J. S. Bach

179. IN ALLEN MEINEN TATEN

J. S. Bach

180. LIEBSTER JESU, WIR SIND HIER

J. S. Bach

181. WACH AUF, MEIN HERZ

J. S. Bach

Two-Voice Compositions

182. WIE SCHÖN LEUCHTET DER MORGENSTERN

J. S. Bach

183. WENN WIR IN HÖCHSTEN NÖTEN SEIN

J. C. Bach

184. CANON IN THE OCTAVE

Prout

185. KOMM, HEILIGER GEIST

Telemann

186. CHORUS NO. 64 from "Judas Maccabaeus"

Handel

187. GLORIA IN EXCELSIS from "Sixteenth Mass"

Haydn

188. DIE NACHTIGAL

Mendelssohn

189. GRUSS

Mendelssohn

190. EIN' FESTE BURG IST UNSER GOTT

J. C. Bach

191. REVERSE RETROGRADE CANON

J. C. Lobe

Unequal Time Durations
in Compound Rhythm

RHYTHMIC READING

The *compound beat** is divided into *three equal time durations.* The reciting syllables for the *compound beat* are "one-lah-lee," "two-lah-lee," etc. Example:

Unequal time durations may occur within the *compound beat,* by tying "one" and "lah" or "lah" and "lee." Example:

The *beat* may be *tied* into the *equal or unequal time durations* of the *compound beat.* Example:

The time values used in this Section are as follows:
1. Symbols indicating the duration of the *compound beat.*
2. Symbols indicating the duration of *two or more compound beats.*
3. Symbols indicating *unequal time durations within the compound beat.*
4. Symbols indicating the durations of *one or more compound beats tied* into the divisions of three of the *compound beat* or the unequal divisions of the *compound beat.*

---

* *Beats* which consistently create the feeling of the division of three produce the *compound beat. Meters* using the *compound beat* create *compound time* 9/8, 9/4, or 9/16 *time signatures* indicate *compound triple meter.*

PITCH RELATIONSHIP

TONIC AND DOMINANT

Major Key

1. DIE KINDESMÖRDERIN

2. THE LINCOLNSHIRE POACHER

3. HUSARENGLAUBE

4. SUR LE BORD DE L'ILE

France

5. NA VAS

Slovakia

6. QUICK! WE HAVE BUT A SECOND *

Ireland

Minor Key

7. FOLK-SONG

Norway

* By permission of Boosey-Hawkes-Belwin, Inc., agent for the copyright owners—Boosey and Company.

8. THE EBB OF THE TIDE

Great Britain

9. ENTREZ, LA BELLE, EN VIGNE

France

SUBDOMINANT AND SUPERTONIC

Major Key

10. GOLDEN SLUMBERS KISS YOUR EYES

England

11. SORRY THE DAY I GOT MARRIED

England

12. AT WINCHESTER WAS A WEDDING

England

13. I'LL NEVER LOVE THEE MORE

Scotland

14. LES METAMORPHOSES

France

15. LA FEMME DU MARIN

France

16. BLYTHE HAVE I BEEN ON YON HILL

17. I'LL NEVER LOVE THEE MORE

18. QUICK! WE HAVE BUT A SECOND *

Minor Key

19. RETURNING

20. DEN SISTE LAURDAGSKVELLEN

Norway

21. FUGUE SUBJECT

Rheinberger

MODULATION TO CLOSELY RELATED KEYS

22. I MADE LOVE TO KATE

England

23. EVENTIDE

Franz

24. THE VIOLET

Andante Con Moto e espressivo

25. THE OYSTER GIRL

In Moderate Time

26. THE APPROACH OF NIGHT

Con Moto

27. ROWING THE ISLA TO MIST

Scotland

28. IN PRAISE OF MILK

England

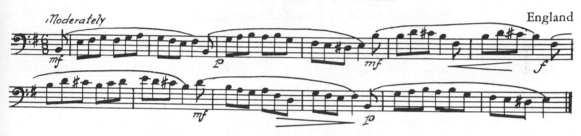

29. THE GIANTS *

Flanders

30. I WANDER THROUGH THE STILL NIGHT

Franz

* By permission of Boosey-Hawkes-Belwin, Inc., agent for the copyright owners—Boosey and Company.

31. CEASE YOUR FUNNING

England

32. KOMM, JESU, KOMM ZU DEINER KIRCHE
From Cantata No. 61

J. S. Bach

33. DER ABSCHIED IM KORBE

Germany

34. DAS LIED VOM JUNGEN GRAFEN

Germany

SIGHT-SINGING MANUAL

QUICKIES
Fugue Subjects

35.

J. S. Bach

36.

W. F. Bach

37.

Marpurg

38.

J. S. Bach

39.

Cherubini

40.

Mendelssohn

41.

Schumann

Themes

42. SONG FROM "RUDDIGORE"

Sullivan

43. SONNTAGSLIED

Mendelssohn

44. ANDENKEN

Beethoven

45. OH BOYS, CARRY ME 'LONG

Foster

46. THEME FROM PIANO TRIO

Mozart

47. DIE BLAUEN FRÜHLINGSAUGEN

Franz

48.

Haydn

TWO-VOICE COMPOSITIONS

49. GIGUE

Handel

50. FROM "THE SEASONS"

Haydn

51. FROM "THE SEASONS"

Haydn

52. GIGA

Valentine Snow

53. FROM "THE SEASONS"

Haydn

54. EXCERPT FROM "QUARTET IN Bb"
Transposed

Mozart

55. LA FOLLETTE

Rameau

18th Century Anonymous

56.

SIGHT-SINGING MANUAL

Subdivision of the Simple Beat

RHYTHMIC READING

The division of the *simple beat* into *four equal time durations* is an elementary subdivision of the *background of two*. The reciting syllables are "one-ta-te-ta," "two-ta-te-ta." Example:

Tying two or three of the four *equal time durations* within the *simple beat* will produce *five unequal time durations* within the *beat*. Example tying the first and second:

Example tying the second and third:*

Example tying the third and fourth:

Example tying the first, second, and third:

* *Syncopation* is created when the *largest duration caused by tying* originates on a *weak pulsation*.

Example tying the second, third, and fourth:*

One – ta Two ta —— One – ta Two ta —— One ta – Two ——

PITCH RELATIONSHIP

TONIC AND DOMINANT

1. ERSTES GRÜN

Schumann

2. DUNCAN GRAY

Scotland

3. FOLK SONG

Ukrainia

---

* *Syncopation* is created when the *largest duration caused by tying* originates on a *weak pulsation.*

4. ZIGEUNERLIEDCHEN

Schumann

5. WIE KOMMT'S, DASS DU SO TRAURIG BIST?

Germany

6. OR DÛEGET OP

The Netherlands

7. FOLK SONG

Ukrainia

8. DIE BROMBEEREN

Germany

9. JOLI DRAGON

France

10. HELLO, GIRLS

United States

SUBDOMINANT AND SUPERTONIC

11. OLD BRASS WAGON

United States

12. I GOT A GAL AT THE HEAD OF THE HOLLER

United States

13. SINCE YOU MEAN TO HIRE FOR SERVICE

Great Britain

14. FRÜHLINGSGLAUBE

Schubert

15. GRACEFUL CONSORT
From "The Creation"

Haydn

16. WEEP NO MORE

Germany

17. I'LL NEVER LEAVE THEE

Great Britain

18. I LIVE NOT WHERE I LOVE

England

19. ALLES STEHT IN GOTTES HAND

Germany

20. DER WASSERMANN

Germany

21. LAULU LAPISTA

22. SERENADE

23. DER JÜNGLING AM BACHE

24. FROM OBERON IN FAIRYLAND

25. IN AUTUMN

Franz

26. WHY BEATS MY HEART SO LOUD?

Franz

27. AWAKE THE HARP
From "The Creation"

Haydn

28. THE LASS OF PATIE'S MILL

Ireland

29. O WERE I ON PARNASSUS HILL

Scotland

30. LORD THOMAS AND FAIR ANNET

Scotland

31. AN DEN MOND

Schubert

32. THE THREE RAVENS

England

Lento espressivo

33. EXPECTATION

Franz

Allegretto

QUICKIES

Fugue Subjects

34.

Fenaroli

Andante

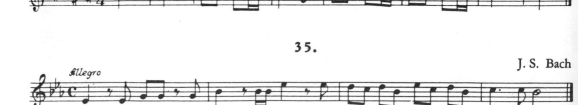

35.

J. S. Bach

Allegro

36.

Mendelssohn

37.

Handel

38.

Hesse

39.

Krebs

40.

Frescobaldi

41.

Mendelssohn

42.

Handel

43.

Ouseley

44.

Frescobaldi

45.

Albrechtsberger

46.

Albrechtsberger

47.

C. P. E. Bach

48.

Mozart

49.

Handel

50. THEME FROM OP. 96

Dvořak

SIGHT-SINGING MANUAL

TWO-VOICE AND THREE-VOICE COMPOSITIONS

51. AGNUS DEI
From Mass No. 18

Mozart

52. AUT MEINEN LIEBEN GOTT

J. N. Hanff

53. HELFT MIR GOTT'S GUTE PREISEN

J. N. Hanff

54. JESU MEINE FREUDE

J. G. Walther

55. EXCERPT FROM MASS IN C, NO. 12

Mozart

56. EXCERPT FROM MASS IN F, NO. 6

Mozart

57. THOU IN THY MERCY
From "Israel in Egypt"

Handel

SIGHT-SINGING MANUAL

58. ER HAT GESAGT

Johann Theile

59. TRAITOR OF LOVE
From "Samson"

Handel

60. CANON

W. F. Bach

61. AIR

Samuel Howard

SIGHT-SINGING MANUAL

62. COME ON THE LIGHT WINGED GALE
Excerpt from a Glee

J. W. Callcott

63. GRAZIE, AGL' INGANNI TUOI*
From "Die Ungetreue Nice"

Mozart

* An example of the tenor part written in the treble clef. The actual sound is an octave lower.

64. EXCERPT FROM "DIE ADVOCATEN"

Schubert

65. EXCERPT FROM "WHEN FAIR BACCHUS FILLS MY BREAST"

Joseph Baildon

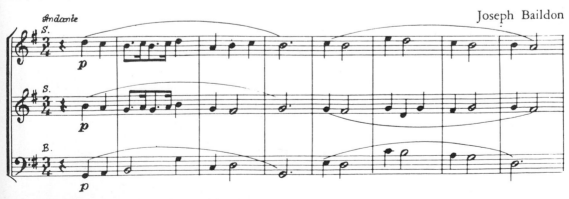

66. TERZETT
From the Cantata, "Dir, Selle des Weltalls"

Mozart

SIGHT-SINGING MANUAL

67. FROM THE CANTATA, "DIE FEIER DES WOHLWOLLENS"

Fr. Kuhlau

SECTION IV

The Tie

A *beat* or a *group of beats* may be *tied* into the *division of a beat.* Examples of *tying into the division of a compound beat:* *

Examples of *tying into the divisions* of a *simple beat:*

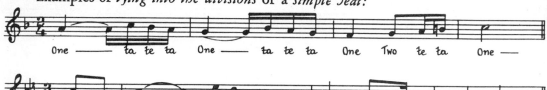

1. TÄUSCHUNG

Schubert

2. GONDOLIER SONG

Mendelssohn

Allegretto non troppo

3. NOW, WELCOME, MY WOOD!

Franz

Vivace

4. LE VOEU PENDANT L'ORAGE

Meyerbeer

Allegro

5. SONG OF SPRING

Mendelssohn

Allegro Vivace

* From here on the rhythmic syllable *lah* will be indicated by *la*.

6. SCHLUMMERLIED

Schubert

7. THE CHARMER

Mendelssohn

8. THEME FROM THE MINUET OF SONATA NO. 36

Haydn

9. DAS ZÜGENGLÖCKLEIN

Schubert

10. EIN KLEINES HAUS

Haydn

11. DAS STRICKENDE MÄDCHEN

Haydn

12. DEN LANGTANDE

Sweden

13. BLACK-EYED SUSAN

R. Leveridge

14. FORTUNE, MY FOE

England

15. GLAUBE, HOFFNUNG UND LIEBE

Schubert

16. IT WAS A LOVER AND HIS LASS

England

SIGHT-SINGING MANUAL

17. AK, HVOR KILDENS VANDE

Poland

18. TRAIL TO MEXICO

United States

19. ERHALT UNS, HERR, BEI DEINEM WORT

Walther

20. O LORD, WHOSE MERCIES NUMBERLESS
From "Saul"

Handel

21. WO FERNE DU DEN EDLEN FRIEDEN
From Cantata No. 41

Bach

22. HOW STANDS THE GLASS AROUND

England

23. TRITT AUF DIE GLAUBENSBAHN
From Cantata No. 152

Bach

24. BE YE SURE THAT THE LORD IS GOD
From the Te Deum and Jubilate in D

Purcell

25. FUGUE SUBJECT

Schicht

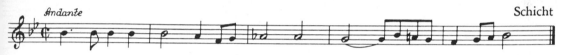

26. FUGUE SUBJECT

Albrechtsberger

27. SPRING, HER LOVELY CHARMS UNFOLDING
From the "Seasons"

Haydn

28. EXCERPT FROM "THE MAGIC FLUTE"

Mozart

SECTION V

Syncopation

The *tie* used in connection with *beats* and *divisions of beats* may produce *syncopation.* Example of *syncopation* produced by *tying beats:*

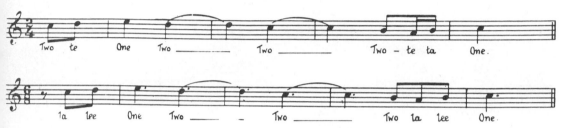

Example of *syncopation* produced by *tying a division of a beat* into *a beat* or *beats:*

Example of *syncopation* produced by *tying a division of a beat* into the *division of another beat:*

One lee Two la lee One la lee One la la lee One

1. HOCHLANDISCHES WIEGENLIED

Schumann

2. CHERRY GATHERING

Hungary

3. VJERNOST DO SMRTI

Slovakia

4. LOTH TO DEPART *

Wales

* By permission of Boosey-Hawkes-Belwin, Inc., agent for the copyright owners—Boosey and Company.

SIGHT-SINGING MANUAL

5. CHILDREN, YOU'LL BE CALLED ON

United States

6. THE MASSACRE AT GLENCOE

Ireland

7. OCH GHEDINK MIJNS

Netherlands

8. MY LORD, WHAT A MORNIN'

United States

9. NUN WIRD MEIN LIEBSTER BRÄUTIGAM
From the "Christmas Oratorio"

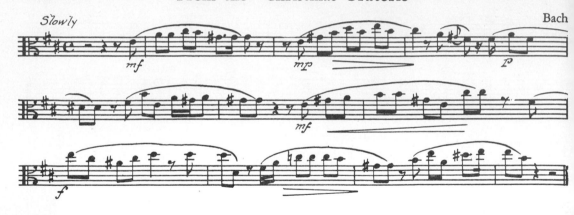

10. HANGMAN

11. MELODY FROM THE FIRST MOVEMENT OF
THE STRING QUARTET, OP. 41

       SIGHT-SINGING MANUAL

12. DANCE A BABY DITTY

England

13. RAMBLING SHOEMAKER

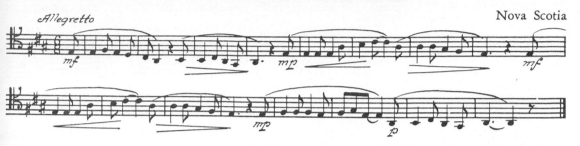

Nova Scotia

14. THE QUAY OF DUNDOCKEN

Newfoundland

15. WER NUR DEN LIEBEN GOTT LÄSST WALTEN

Bach

16. WOHL EUCH, IHR AUSERWÄHLTEN SEELEN
From Cantata No. 34

Bach

17. WALK, MARY, DOWN DE LANE

United States

18. CALVARY

United States

19. JEGENYEFA TETEJÉBE

Hungary

20. DO DON'T TOUCH-A MY GARMENT, GOOD LORD, I'M GWINE HOME

United States

21. CAN'T YOU LIVE HUMBLE?

United States

22. O ROCKS, DON'T FALL ON ME

United States

23. GOD'S A-GWINE TER TROUBLE DE WATER

United States

24. MANY THOUSAND GONE

25. BY AN' BY

26. RISE, MOURNER, RISE

27. FOR THE LORD IS A MIGHTY GOD
From the Ninety-fifth Psalm

* This may be sung as a canon, the second voice entering at *

98   SIGHT-SINGING MANUAL

QUICKIES

Fugue Subjects

28.

Klengel

29.

Pepusch

30.

Klengel

31.

Handel

32.

Marpurg

33.

A. W. Marchant

34.

Langsam   Leonardo Leo

35.

Andante   Guilmant

36.

Allegro   J. C. Bach

37.

Adagio   Ouseley

38.

Andante   Mozart

39.

Andante   C. P. E. Bach

40.

Andante   Handel

41.

Sala

42.

Albrechtsberger

43.

Handel

44.

Albrechtsberger

45.

Rheinberger

Themes

46.

Bruckner

47.

Brahms

Allegro ma non troppo

48.

Dvorak, Op. 96

Allegro ma non troppo

TWO-VOICE COMPOSITIONS

49. DUET NO. 18
From "Dido and Aeneas"

Purcell

Allegro non troppo

mf

50. HALLELUJAH CHORUS
From "The Mount of Olives"

Beethoven

51. DUET: AT LAST, DEAR, I FIND YOU ALONE
From "Fidelio"

Beethoven

52. CHORUS: DAS NEUE REGIMENT
From Cantata No. 71 "Gott Ist Mein König"

J. S. Bach

53. SONNTAGSMORGEN

Mendelssohn

54. O, WHAT PLEASURES, PAST EXPRESSING
From "Alexander Balus"

Handel

SIGHT-SINGING MANUAL

55. GOTT, DU HAST ES WOHL GEFÜGET
From Cantata No. 63

J. S. Bach

56. WE BELIEVE THAT THOU SHALT COME
From the Chandos Te Deum

Handel

57. CHORUS: O LORD, IN THEE HAVE I TRUSTED
From Te Deum Laudamus

Graun

58. FOR MY RASHNESS THOU MUST PERISH
From "Die Entfuhrung aus dem Serail"

Mozart

59. DUET: WE THEREFORE PRAY
From Te Deum Laudamus

Graun

SIGHT-SINGING MANUAL

60. SHE PUT ON RIGHTEOUSNESS
From "The Ways Of Zion Do Mourn"

Handel

61. CANON

W. F. Bach

62. THE GLORIOUS COMPANY OF THE APOSTLES PRAISE THEE
From Te Deum

Handel

63. EXCERPT FROM "ATHALIA," OP. 74

Mendelssohn

64. THEY SHALL RECEIVE A GLORIOUS CROWN
From "The Ways Of Zion Do Mourn"

Handel

65. WENN SORGEN AUF MICH DRINGEN
From Canata No. 3, "Ach Gott, Wie Manches Herzeleid"

J. S. Bach

SIGHT-SINGING MANUAL

66. KYRIE ELEISON
From "Mass in B Minor"

J. S. Bach

67. DOMINE DEUS
From "Mass in B Minor"

J. S. Bach

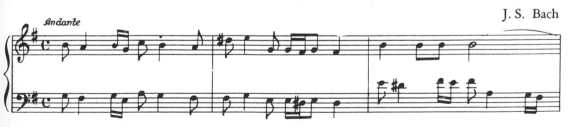

68. QUARTET, OP. 18, No. 4 *

Beethoven

69. THEME FROM A QUARTET

Schumann

70. AUS TIEFER NOT

Pachelbel

* This is double counterpoint at the octave. Repeat inverting voices.

71. DUO

Telemann

72. CANON AT THE SECOND ABOVE AND SIXTH BELOW

Mozart

SECTION VI

Superimposed Backgrounds and Superimposed Meter

SUPERIMPOSED BACKGROUNDS

Time durations based upon the *compound beat* may be introduced in *simple meter.*
When this occurs, use the reciting syllable for the *compound beat.* Example:

Time durations based upon the *simple beat* may be introduced in *compound meter.*
When this occurs, use the reciting syllables for the *simple beat.* Example:

SUPERIMPOSED METER

Occasionally the *time duration* of an *established simple meter* may have *another*
simple meter superimposed upon it. For example:

This is in reality a *3/4 meter* in the *same time duration* as that of the *2/4 meter.*
The rhythmic syllables for the 2/4 ♩♩♩ should be those used for the 3/4 ♩♩♩
Example:

SIGHT-SINGING MANUAL

1. FOLK SONG

Grieg

Con Moto

2. THEME FROM THE "ROMANTIC SYMPHONY," SECOND MOVEMENT*

Howard Hanson

Andante

3. MELODY

Allen McHose

4. ET RESURREXIT
From the Third Mass

Haydn

Vivace

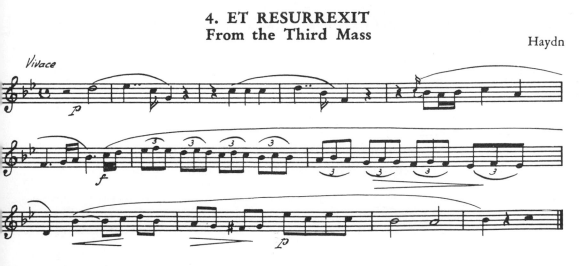

*From *Romantic Symphony* by Howard Hanson. Copyright 1932 by the Eastman School of Music. International copyright secured.

5. TO SPRING

Grieg

6. EXCERPT FROM "MERRY MOUNT," ACT II, SCENE 1*

Howard Hanson

7. MELODY FROM "PAN AND THE PRIEST"

Howard Hanson

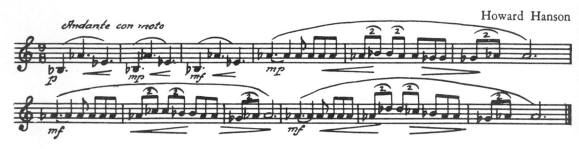

8. I SAID OF LAUGHTER, IT IS MAD
From "Beyond These Voices is Peace"

Parry

* From *Merry Mount* by Howard Hanson. Copyright 1933—Harms, Inc.

9. EXCERPT FROM "MERRY MOUNT," ACT I*

Howard Hanson

10. THEME FROM THE "ROMANTIC SYMPHONY," FIRST MOVEMENT†

Howard Hanson

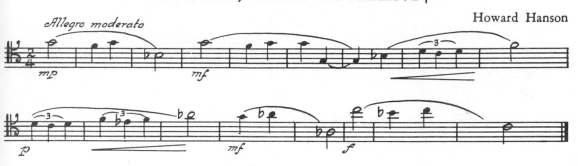

11. THEME FROM THE "ROMANTIC SYMPHONY," THIRD MOVEMENT†

Howard Hanson

12. THEME

Brahms

---

* From *Merry Mount* by Howard Hanson. Copyright 1933—Harms, Inc.

† From *Romantic Symphony* by Howard Hanson. Copyright 1932 by the Eastman School of Music. International copyright secured.

13. FUGUE SUBJECT

Merkel

14. DER TOD JESU, NO. 12

Graun

SIGHT-SINGING MANUAL

Subdivision of the Background

The *background* of a *simple beat* or *compound* beat may be divided into two, three, or four equal *time durations*. The *simple beat* subdivided into *four equal time durations* was explained in Section III.

The *simple beat* may also be subdivided into *six equal time durations*. Example:

The *simple beat* may also be subdivided into *eight equal time durations*. Example:

The *compound beat* may also be subdivided into *six equal time durations*. Example:

The compound beat may also be subdivided into *nine equal time durations*. Example:

The *compound beat* may also be subdivided into *twelve equal time durations*. Example:

The use of the *tie* within the subdivided *simple* or *compound beats* produces man[y] *unequal time durations*. The five examples which follow show a few *unequal time dura[tions]* and their reciting syllables:

1. IN LOVE SHOULD THERE MEET

Great Britain

2. THERE WAS A LADY IN THE WEST

England

3. DE MA PREMIÈRE AMIE

Meyerbeer

4. OLUF'S BALLAD

Gade

5. HAVFRUENS SPAADOM

Denmark

6. A HEALTH TO ALL HONEST MEN

England

7. GREVEN OG KONGEDATTEREN

Denmark

8. MEIN JESU, ZIEHE MICH NACH DIR
From Cantata No. 22

Bach

9. GIVE EAR TO A FROLICSOME DITTY

England

10. AN DEN MOND

Schubert

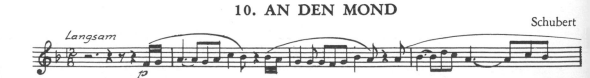

11. SEI GEGRUSSET, JESU GÜTIG (VAR. VII)

Bach

12. BENEATH THE CYPRESS
From "Susanna"

Handel

13. HÖCHSTER, HÖCHSTER, MACHE DEINE GÜTE
From Cantata No. 51

Bach

14. MOTHER, OH SING ME TO REST!

Franz

15. I WONDER WHAT THOU'RT DOING

Franz

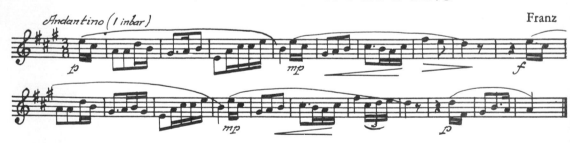

16. CARO FIGLIO, AMATO DIO
From "La Resurrezione"

Handel

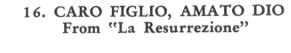

17. ALL BEAUTY WITHIN YOU

Italy

18. AND THE ROSES, THEY FLOURISH

Franz

19. FOLK SONG

Ukrainia

20. THE LAST ROSE

Franz

21. DES MÄDCHENS KLAGE

Schubert

22. AN DIE SONNE

Schubert

23. DER SCHATZGRÄBER

Schubert

SIGHT-SINGING MANUAL

24. IDENS NACHTGESANG

Schubert

25. DAS HEIMWEH

Schubert

26. LA SCILLITANA

Italy

27. DER ALPENJÄGER

Schubert

28. FOLK SONG

Ukrainia

29. ÚGY ELMEGYEK, MEGLÁTJÁTOK

Hungary

30. MERKT UND HÖRT, IHR MENSCHENKINDER
From Cantata No. 7

Bach

SIGHT-SINGING MANUAL

31. HERR CHRIST, DER EIN'GE GOTT'SSOHN

Buxtehude

Adagio

32. EXCERPT FROM "MERRY MOUNT," ACT II, SCENE 3*

Howard Hanson

* From *Merry Mount* by Howard Hanson. Copyright 1933—Harms, Inc.

FUGUE SUBJECTS

33.

Andante   Padre Martini

34.

Moderato   Padre Martini

35.

Andante   J. S. Bach

36.

Andante   Merkel

THEMES

37.

Andante   Haydn

38. FROM OP. 96

Lento   Dvorak

39.

TWO-VOICE COMPOSITIONS

40. LET'S IMITATE HER NOTES ABOVE
From "Alexander's Feast"

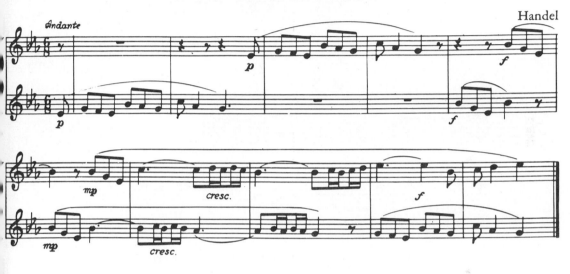

41. WER MICH LIEBET, DER WIRD MEIN WORT HALTEN
From Cantata No. 74

42. HE DOTH TO ME INCLINE
From "Fidelio"

Beethoven

43. IN ISRAEL'S CAMP ALONE I WEEP
From "Moses in Egypt"

Rossini

SIGHT-SINGING MANUAL

18th Century

45. GLORIA
From Mass No. 6

Mozart

18th Century, Anonymous

47. WIE KANN ICH FROH UND LUSTIG SEIN?

Mendelssohn

SIGHT-SINGING MANUAL

48. CANON

J. P. Kirnberger

SECTION VIII

Remote Modulation

1. HÖK OCH DUFVA

Sweden

2. PLEASING PAINS

Haydn

3. TROST IN TRÄNEN

Schubert

4. DAS WIRTSHAUS

Schubert

5. NACHT UND TRAUME

Schubert

6. SILENT SAFETY

Franz

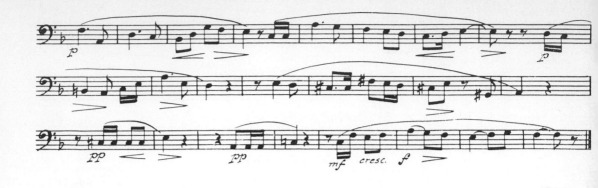

7. SPRING'S APPROACH

Franz

8. SUMMERTIME

Franz

9. DESPAIR

Haydn

10. THE SEASON COMES WHEN FIRST
WE MET (RECOLLECTION)

Haydn

SECTION IX

The Divided Beat

The *meter signature* does not always indicate the *nature of the conductor's beat.* The *tempo indication* and the *nature of the composition* strongly influence the selection of the *conductor's beat.* It is frequently altered to satisfactorily control a large group of performers in *rallentandos, ritardandos,* etc. The method used to achieve the solution of such problems is the *divided beat.* The *simple beat* is divided into two parts, and the *compound beat* into three parts. Two examples follow.

2/4 meter with a *tempo indication Largo* is conducted as follows:

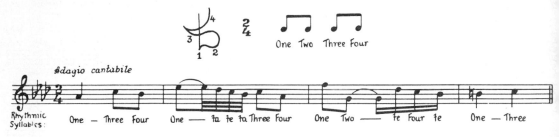

6/8 meter with a *tempo indication Lento* is conducted as follows:

For further information concerning the divided beat refer to Part I of *Basic Principles of the Technique of 18th and 19th Century Composition,* by Allen McHose.

1. WITH VERDURE CLAD
From "The Creation"

2. SYMPATHY

Haydn

3. FAREWELL, FAREWELL! YE LIMPID SPRINGS AND FLOODS
From "Jephthah"

Handel

4. WER NUR DEN LIEBEN GOTT LÄSST WALTEN

Bach

5. YE SONS OF ISRAEL From "Samson"

Handel

6. RETURN, RETURN, O GOD OF HOSTS From "Samson"

Handel

7. O GOD, HAVE MERCY From "St. Paul"

Mendelssohn

8. GEDULD, GEDULD! From the "St. Matthew Passion"

Bach

SECTION X

Chromaticism

FUGUE SUBJECTS

1.

21.

Kirnberger

22.

Rheinberger

23.

Rheinberger

24.

Rheinberger

TWO-VOICE AND THREE-VOICE COMPOSITIONS

25. ICH WOLLT' MEINE LIEB' ERGÖSSE SICH, OP. 63, NO. 1

Mendelssohn

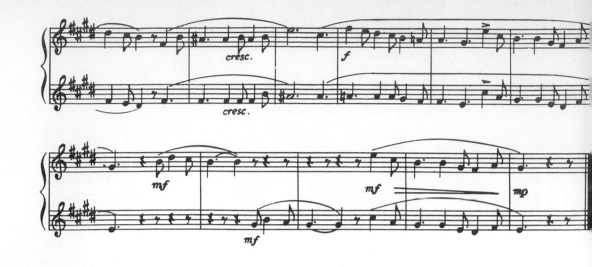

26. DUET: MY SON, BEWARE OF WOMAN'S FALSEHOOD
From "The Magic Flute"

Mozart

27. CATCH

J. W. Callcott

SIGHT-SINGING MANUAL

28. CANON

Mozart

* This part may be performed by a student on either the piano, cello, or bassoon.

29. THREE-VOICE CANON

Mozart

30. WHERE WEEPING YEWS
Excerpt from an Elegy

Francis Ireland (1773)

31. TAFELLIED, OP. 93 B

Brahms

32. CANON A 2 (CRAB CANON)
From "The Musical Offering"

J. S. Bach

33. DUET: I LOVE THE LORD
From "David in the Wilderness"

Beethoven

SECTION XI

Modal Melodies

1. BOTANY BAY

England

2. WEISS KEIN BESS'RES LAGER MIR

Hungary

3. VATER UNSER IM HIMMELREICH

Martin Luther

4. TISZA PARTJAN VAN EGY

Hungary

5. HEAR THE BELLS PEALING

Moderately fast   Russia

6. BESSEY BELL AND MARY GRAY

Lively   Great Britain

7. ACH GOTT, VOM HIMMEL SIEH' DAREIN

Melody from Erfurter Enchiridion, 1524

Allegretto

8. AND GIN YE MEET A BONNY LASSIE

Moderately   Scotland

9. FATHME

Algiers

10. AUS TIEFER NOT SCHREI' ICH ZU DIR

Melody from Walter's Geystliche Gesangk Büchleyn, 1524

11. DANDSEVISE

Russia

12. THE DUKE OF ARGYLE

Newfoundland

SIGHT-SINGING MANUAL

13. LORD THOMAS

England

14. SUMMERTIME

Minnesinger, 13th Century

15. UNGER SVENS SORG

Sweden

16. RELIGION IS A FORTUNE, I REALLY DO BELIEVE

United States

17. THE THREE RAVENS

Scotland

18. ANCIENT MELODY

C. 1615

19. COULD'ST THOU ONLY SEE ME NOW

Franz

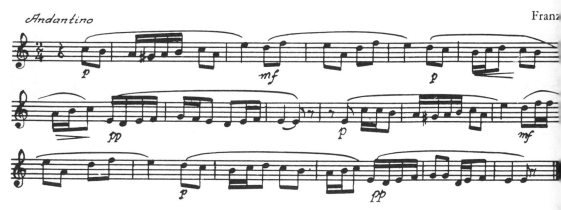

20. SIX JOLLY MINERS

United States

21. OLD SIMON THE KING

Gaily England

22. DANS PARIS YA-T-UNE BRUNE PLUS BELLE QUE LE JOUR

Moderately Canada

23. MY JO JANET

Great Britain

Andantino

24. THE GABERLUNZIE MAN

Great Britain

Slowly

25. LORD RONALD

26. ONNETON NUORNKAINEN

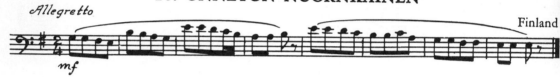

27. SHALL I GO WALK THE WOODS SO WILD?

28. EWE-BUGHTS MARION

SIGHT-SINGING MANUAL

29. AH! THE SIGHS THAT COME FRO' THE HEART

30. OH, LADDIE WITH THE GOLDEN HAIR

31. AS I ROVED OUT

32. THE POOR MAN'S RESOLUTION

33. AVENGING AND BRIGHT

SECTION XI

34. LA PASIÓN

Spain

35. FLYING, FLYING HIGH O'ER HILL AND DALE

Russia

36. JOHN BARLEYCORN

England

37. BY YON CASTLE WA'

Scotland

38. THE PRETTY GIRL MILKING HER COW

Ireland

39. SILDIG ANGER

Bohemia

40. ON THE SEA FLOATING WENT A SHELDUCK GRAY

Russia

41. MY NAME IT IS JACK

Scotland

42. WREATH OF GOLD IN HAND

Russia

SIGHT-SINGING MANUAL

SECTION XII

Less Common Meter Signatures and Mixed Meters

LESS COMMON METER SIGNATURES

Simple and compound meters of five, six, seven, or more *beats* are less frequent in the music of the 18th Century, but by the close of the 19th Century and the advent of the 20th they assume a position of importance. In *simple meter* the upper number of the *meter signature* is 5, 6, 7, etc. In *compound meter* the upper number is 15, 18, 21, etc.

The rhythmic reading syllables for these meters are illustrated in these two examples:

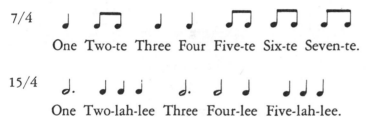

7/4   One Two-te Three Four Five-te Six-te Seven-te.

15/4   One Two-lah-lee Three Four-lee Five-lah-lee.

The conventional *conductor's beat* for these meters is explained in Part I of *Basic Principles of the Technique of 18th and 19th Century Composition* by Allen McHose, or in *Handbook of Conducting* by Karl Van Hoesen.

MIXED METERS

The term *mixed meters* is applied to different *meters* which follow each other in close succession. The resulting *measures* are of *different time durations.* Two conditions usually maintain in *mixed* meter passages: (1) *beat equals beat* when the *meter* changes; and (2) *background of beat remains constant* when the meter changes. Example of *beat equals beat:*

One te Two Three te Four   One te Two te Three te Four te · One Two Three

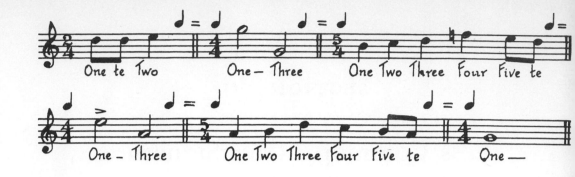

Example of *background of beat remaining constant:*

1. WENN UNSRE BURSCHEN SINGEN

Finland

2. THEME FROM THE SIXTH SYMPHONY, SECOND MOVEMENT

Tschaikowsky

3. LASTA TUUDITTAESSA

Moderato   Finland

4. APPEARANCES

Andantino   Russia

5. COSSACK SONG

Presto   Russia

6. HOME MY SWEETHEART COMES FROM ROVING

With expression   Finland

7. NOW, WILL NOT HE SOMETIMES IN THINKING?

With deep emotion   Franz

8. VERZWEIFLUNG

Croatia

9. MUTTER SO ZÄRTLICH MICH LIEBTE

Bulgaria

10. ON MY VINEYARD GREEN

Russia

11. LA PORQUEYROLA

Slovakia

12. WHEN I STILL WAS A YOUNG LADDIE

Hungary

SIGHT-SINGING MANUAL

13. HESTENE PAA BRAKMARKEN

Bohemia

14. THE SAD AGED BOUGHS

Hungary

15. GEVINSTEN

Bohemia

16. EGER TOWN IS ON A FINE PLACE

Hungary

17. A PRETTY MAID MILKING HER GOAT

United States

18. SVAKO DJELO KONAC IMA

Slovakia

19. LA BERGÈRE

Netherlands

20. LA VIOLETTE DOUBLE

France

SIGHT-SINGING MANUAL

21. THE MESSENGER NIGHTINGALE

22. JOHNNY ON HIS SOFA

23. LA DAMA DE ARAGÓN

24. LÁSKA VOJÍNOVA

25. ISTA PJESMA

Slovakia

26. NEMILI

Slovakia

27. ISABEAU S'Y PROMÈNE

Canada

28. CANSÓ DE NADAL

Spain

Sight-Singing Manual

29. INAČICA

Slovakia

30. J'AI PERDU MON AMANT

Canada

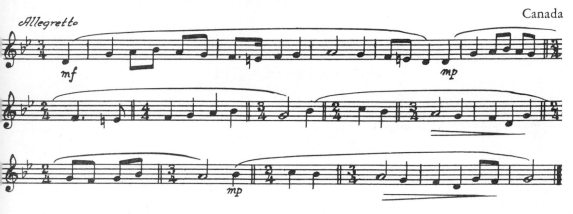

31. FROM THE FOREST GREEN

Russia

32. VZADÁLENÁ

Bohemia

33. LA DAMA DE ARAGÓN

Spain

34. THE DESERTER'S PLAINT

France

35. KIMIAD ANN ENE

Brittany

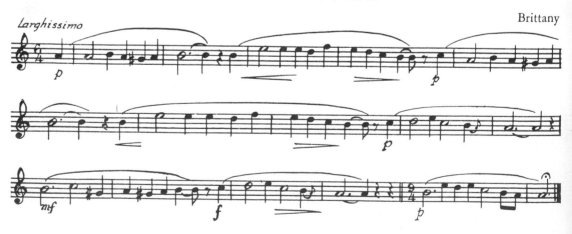

SIGHT-SINGING MANUAL

36. METAMORPHOSIS

France

Moderato

37. EXCERPT FROM "PAN AND THE PRIEST"

Howard Hanson

38. CERCLES MYSTERIEUX DES ADOLESCENTS*
From "Le Sacre du Printemps"

Stravinsky

39. LES PRINCES ROYAUX DE KRAKOW

Russia

* By permission of Edition Russe de Musique, Paris. Agents in the United States, Galaxy Music Corporation, New York.

40. EXCERPT FROM "MERRY MOUNT," ACT I*

Howard Hanson

41. ROYAL MARCH
From "L'Histoire du Soldat"

Stravinsky

SIGHT-SINGING MANUAL

SECTION XIII

Sixteenth and Seventeenth Century
Part Music

1. VERSET: INTER INÍQUOS

Palestrina

* The instructor may select the opening dynamics according to his taste.

2. VERSET: TRADIDIT IN MORTEM

Palestrina

3. VERSET: TANQUAM AGNUS

Victoria

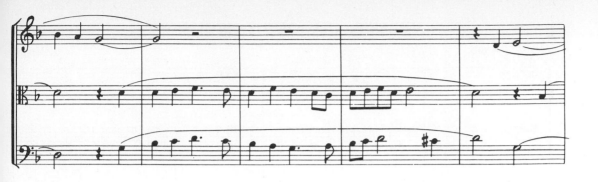

4. VERSET: QUID DORMITIS?

Victoria

5. VERSET: CUMQUE INJECISSENT

Victoria

6. CANON

William Byrd

SIGHT-SINGING MANUAL

7. CANZONET 3

Morley

SIGHT-SINGING MANUAL

8. CANZONET 15

Morley

9. CANZONET 19

Morley

10. EXCERPT FROM THE ORATORIO, "JEPHTE"

Carissini

11. EXCERPT FROM THE ORATORIO, "JONAS"

Carissini

12. WIR GLAUBEN ALL AN EINEN GOTT

Scheidt

SECTION XIII

183

13. MISSA I, SUPER DIXIT MARIA

Hassler

14. WAS MENSCHEN KRAFFT (2nd Part)

Schiedt

15. CHRISTUM WIR SOLLEN LOBEN SCHON

Scheidt

SIGHT-SINGING MANUAL

PSALMUS: DA JESUS AN DEM KREUZE STUND

Scheidt

16. CHRIST LAG IN TODESBANDEN

F. W. Zachau

17. DIALOGUE

Scheidt

SIGHT-SINGING MANUAL